The Little Book of
VALENTINE'S DAY

By Zack Bush and Laurie Friedman
Illustrated by Sarah Van Evera

DEDICATED TO YOU —
OUR WONDERFUL READER.

THIS BOOK BELONGS TO:

_____

VALENTINE'S DAY is the perfect holiday to tell all of the special people in your life just how much they mean to you!

And there are so many fun, creative ways you can do it.
Ready for some **VALENTINE'S DAY**
tips, tricks, and secrets? Just turn the page!

A good place to begin is by making a list.
You can include anyone on yours who you
want to celebrate on **VALENTINE'S DAY.**

Your family.

Your friends.

Your teacher. Even special people in your community.

Who would you put on your list?

AUNT

COUSIN

BABY-SITTER

UNCLE

FRIEND

TEACHER

There are so many things you can do to make this **VALENTINE'S DAY** unforgettable.

Making cards is easy and lots of fun!
All you need is some paper, markers or crayons,
and any other art supplies you want to use.

And, of course,
a grown-up to help!

VALENTINE'S DAY is all about **LOVE**, which means lots and lots of **HEARTS**.

Here's a trick for making your own.

Step one:
Fold a piece of
construction paper in half.

Step two:
Draw half a **HEART**
on one side of the paper.

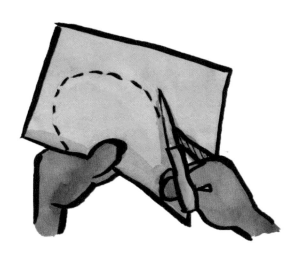

Step three:
Cut along the line.

Step four:
Open it up and ta-da . . .
a perfect **HEART!**

You can write on your **HEARTS**, decorate your **HEARTS**, or glue your **HEARTS** together.

Whatever you decide to do, everyone will love getting
VALENTINE'S DAY cards made by you!

There are so many other ways to make
VALENTINE'S DAY extra special.

You can bake cookies . . .
and share them with people you **LOVE**.

You can pick flowers . . .
and give them to someone special.

You can make bracelets . . .
and exchange them with a close friend.

One of the most fun things to do on **VALENTINE'S DAY**
is to play games with your friends and family.

HEART beanbag toss.

HEART hopscotch.

HEART tic-tac-toe.

Or a **VALENTINE'S DAY** game of Cupid's arrow toss.

You can also use your words on **VALENTINE'S DAY.**
There are so many special ones to choose from.

That's a good way of telling someone
that you are filled with **LOVE** for them!

"Let's have a heart-to-heart talk."

If you say that to another person who wants to talk,
it shows them how much you care.

"Even though you are far away,
you are always in my heart."

When
the people
you
aren't nearby, this
is a great way to tell
them just how much
you miss and   them.

And some days you just need to remind yourself to
listen to your heart about which direction you should go.

Still not sure what you want to do
to celebrate **VALENTINE'S DAY**?

You can share some **VALENTINE'S DAY** candy.

You can make special VALENTINE'S DAY treats.

You can make a **VALENTINE'S DAY** promise to be best friends forever.

And remember . . . the best **VALENTINE'S DAY**
gift of all is always a hug and a kiss.

CONGRATULATIONS!

You've earned your

VALENTINE'S DAY BADGE.

Now you know so many great ways

to make **VALENTINE'S DAY** extra special!

Go to the website
www.BooksByZackAndLaurie.com
to print out your Valentine's Day badge
from the Printables & Activities page.

And if you like this book, please go to
Amazon and leave a kind review.

Keep reading all of the books in
#thelittlebookof
series to learn new things
and earn more badges.

Other books in the series include:

The Little Book of Camping
The Little Book of Friendship
The Little Book of Kindness
The Little Book of Presidential Elections
The Little Book of Giving
The Little Book of Patience
The Little Book of Government

Made in the USA
Monee, IL
07 January 2021